Foreword

Just over a year ago I met a lady called Peggy Rowett through a friend. Peggy had recently lost her daughter, Yvonne, who had suffered a difficult life and whose constant struggle against suffering was an inspiration to Peggy and her family.

Peggy asked me if I could help turn some of her memories of her daughter Yvonne into a written memoir. What follows then is (from Peggy's point of view and through my words) a sense of Yvonne's life, her bravery and a glimpse of how she suffered from never fully being given the care she needed.

There is no blame here, just a wish for people to understand more deeply, and a hope that society will grow to be able to include all, even those that don't quite fit in...

I hope it means something to you.

Benjamin Symes

NB Part of the proceeds of the sale of the book will go to support the Merlin Project (details of which can be found at the end).

Thanks to my dad for his elegant drawings. And thanks to Cav for all that she is.

Shatterings

A lovely summer day, August 23rd 1952. Anticipation. Excitement. Fear. Hope. Love.

And a different day, May 17th 2011. Release. Guilt. Anguish. Hope. Love.

— • —

"Tony?"
"Yes, love."
"I'm scared.."
"I know."

I am young, I cannot wait. Tony loves me, we cannot wait. I can feel her.

And then the telephone rings. And now when I put the receiver to my ear, Tony's younger brother Peter is dead. Killed on his motorbike.

One month.

And here she is. Yvonne. My baby. My longed for beautiful baby girl. My daughter, Yvonne.

(And sometimes they say that's what did it, it's not your fault, it was the trauma, it's not your fault).

I am protecting her and I cannot protect her.

Anyway she's fine. A normal baby girl, a normal little girl. Quite normal. She is headstrong, wilful, strong of spirit. This is who she is. She is Yvonne, my daughter.

"Not those shoes Mummy."
"They're lovely though. What's the matter with them? I thought you liked them."
"I love them. But not today. They're not the same colour as my dress."

Brothers and sisters come. Barbara then Malcolm then Sally then Antony. Yvonne the eldest. Yvonne no longer the bearer of all my love. Yvonne only just ahead, struggling to keep ahead, to be the eldest. She skips with her sister Barbara in the playground with ribbons in her hair.

Her sister Barbara says she is bossy.

She's not doing very well at school. Not the bottom of the class but she's struggling a little. It doesn't seem to mean very much. And anyway it's nothing compared to the animals. Nothing compared to Mischief our spaniel, and all the tiny birds.

She is training Mischief to be less mischievous! They are winning medals together. A team.

And she breeds little budgies. And finches. Their beautiful colours, their precise lines and definitions. Her pride in their appearance. Their fragility. Her careful tending. Her full of care. She is a child.

Then massacre. No.

MASSACRE - 'General and unnecessary slaughter'.

The rats got in and killed them all. Their delicate feathers matted, their tiny bodies twisted, confusion in their eyes. Their lives broken.

And the phone rings. And her first boyfriend, Ali, is dead. Killed on a motorbike.
And the doorbell rings. And Mischief is dead. Killed by a car.
I cannot explain. I cannot explain. I cannot explain. I try to explain.

She's working at the Vets now. And she adopts FiFi, a little black cat with no tail. And she will not go into the butcher's as she cannot look at the carcasses on display. She has a great love. Compassion for all living things. She sees their predicaments, wants to comfort. She is always the last to leave.

"Let me stroke him a little longer."
"It's time Yvonne."
"Just give him 5 more minutes. He's so happy here."

But she can't save them all, her hand the last warmth, the last living connection before thin cold hard sterilized steel and liquid death. Puppies and Kittens. Trusting, tiny, and unaware.

— • —

And here is Yvonne. My baby girl. My daughter. Trusting, tiny and unaware. Death surrounds her.

— • —

She's not very happy. She draws in. Away. Something is wrong. My unhappy girl. We are unhappy. I take her to our family doctor.

"My recommendation is that she stops working there. That she does something quite different."
She is in the room as he talks about her. Disconnected.

— • —

Yvonne is an adult. Eighteen. "I want to go to Looe."

She gets a job in a hotel in Looe. Tony and I take her, get her settled into her little room. We all sit down and work out her days off, when she can come home. We take her away from us. But not far. It's not far. It's not too far.

"She'll be okay, won't she? Everyone seems very nice."
Tony doesn't speak. He drives. He looks in the mirror.

"Tony?...."
"I hope so."

— • —

Bad trip.

Bad.

Trip.

She's experimenting. Smoking pot. Marijuana. And LSD. She wants to get high. Jim Morrison sings:

> "Ghosts crowd the young child's
> Fragile egg-shell mind."

Yvonne cracks. And the cracks extend across the earth, under the soles of our feet.

She peers through the cracks, she peeks cheekily. And she hides herself in the cracks. The precious things. She pushes on, caving, following the sound. And she loses the way back. She folds in on herself, inside out, exposed. She unzips. She is unzipped. She is flirting. Fully naked for anyone to see. I cannot look. My husband's heart hurts.

And all the other children are looking on but they don't see. And neither do we. We only see how she moves, hear her words. We feel how she sometimes flicks violence. How she easily shatters and scatters threats and yet.

And yet.
And yet, she is still the same.
Yvonne. Playing in the rockpools.
Yvonne the big sister, on the beach. Always the eldest, the first and the last.

But we cannot see the twisting snakes within her, the twin degradation of spine and mind.
Hissing psychosis. Multiple sclerosis. Yet to arrive, or for us to have spied.

First Psychosis. Not as familiar as the big C. More sinister, more a disturbance than a disease.
Not the big C, but the silent P. How apt.

But all this unknown, and only known when known too late.

And suddenly she has drifted...

...we have drifted...

apart...

The wonder years.

Movement movement restlessness movement and sometimes there is hope in the calm.
The farm.

"I think they really love her there." Tony reassures me.
I am reassured.

A glimpse. Just a glimpse.
The animals, the good home cooked food, the family, the open spaces, the air.

But the work is hard for her, too hard. And she steps out and on again.

Rolling. Dropping. Sliding. Falling into London where she stands as a nanny.

She is good with children. Kind always kind and generous. And her brothers and sisters love her.
Big family days. But she is scary. Sometimes she is scary.

Perhaps she is scared I think. She wears bright red lipstick and rouge on her cheeks.
Bizarre I think. Like a mask.

Where have you gone Yvonne?
Where are you when you are here but not here?

You get so close to people, close enough for them to love you. And then you slip away.
You sleep rough and each time we've had enough. But I know we'll always take more.

"I've bought her a tent" Tony announces. Quietly.
"At least she will have some shelter".

And gradually and gradually and gradually. Gradually we accept Yvonne is this, and not what we wanted her to be. She comes home again again again and always we hope again but she always separates, leaving leaving leaving, trailing our despair.

She keeps opening herself to all, her body. She keeps giving herself away. She loves deeply.
She gives too much away.

"Tony she is destroying her life." I don't need to tell him.

She joins a cult. A mission. External inhibition. The Divine Light. An ashram.
In South East Cornwall then in London.

One day she sits in her room, blanket over her head. Mind changing. For us all.
"Have you seen God yet?" her youngest brother Antony shouts. She doesn't reply.

And now Tony is ill. How can we not blame? How can we not despair? He is 48 and he has bowel cancer. He is dying.

We need to look after him, we need to focus on him, I cannot cope Yvonne, leave me alone, change, stop doing that, please please come back, I cannot cope, please help. Look at your dad. Please leave, please be different, please be still, please don't, please. I cannot cope. Yvonne.

"I love you Tony." He knows.
"I love you". I know.

Barbara and Malcolm and so many carers, so much care, so much love, so much pain.

Tony dies. He is 49.

— • —

Yvonne is angry with me. So angry. She visits and we walk on the beach. And then she turns on me and I have to run. I am frightened, running away from my big little girl. I protect myself in a phone box, call my son who comes to save me. He drives her back.

He often drives her back, and she threatens to leap from the car.
And somehow life goes on, and we are who we are who we are..

— • —

We are told now that she has a personality disorder. Not a mental illness. A disorder. Impossible to treat. She is the way she is. Disordered. With no chance of finding her way home.

"Don't let her in" - They say.
"You cannot help. If she gets into trouble there is help. Don't attempt to have her at home."

She turns up. Ringing the doorbell, knocking then banging on the door. And we are hiding from our own daughter sister. Hid in a room upstairs, not facing this. But I am her mother. And I will always let her in. She always has another chance. I am her mother. And she is still the same. And still there is more fear and trouble. I have no choice but to let her in.

"Don't let her in. If she gets into trouble there is help."

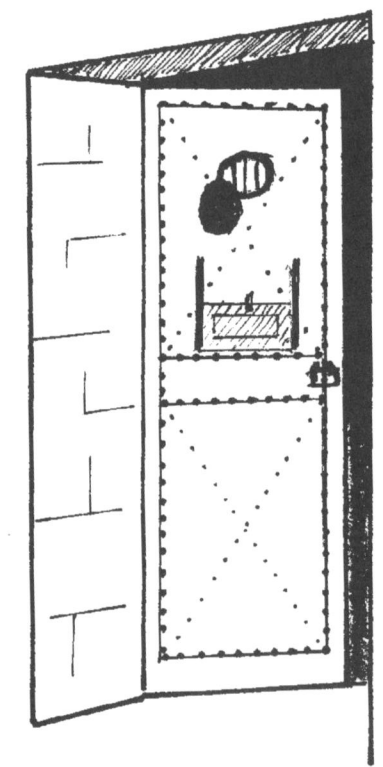

They take her to prison. I see our local MP.

"But we can't just lock people up if they have a personality disorder." he says.
"But you do lock them up. They go to prison."

So they can't lock people up to keep them safe. They lock people up to keep others safe. Basic. Maths.

— • —

Yvonne is a mother. Once twice three times. Four five six times.
Jonathan, Felicity, Lee-Anne, Melanie, Leah-Faye, Jenna.

I hope. I hope that her little one, her first little one, will calm her down, settle her, focus her unkempt loving. I get all the stuff: nappies, pram, a moses basket. This will help.

She is in hospital.
"If you don't get me out of here right now you will never see your grandchild again."

We take her back to her cottage where she is living. The next day she is sectioned.

The baby Jonathan stays with us but I'm not stable enough. We're not a stable stable. Jonathan is fostered and then adopted. And then a year later baby Felicity and then two years later baby Lee-Anne....

Then New Year's Eve 1981. Baby Melanie. She keeps Melanie, allowed to look after her, in more settled surroundings. One month we hold our breath. Two months. Three months. And then Melanie has to be adopted. Yvonne's erratic life.

Then baby Leah. Again we try. We try. 9 months later and it's too risky. Leah is at risk. Yvonne has bruised her cheek. We desperately try to get help. Social Services. No one home. Yvonne gets drunk. Leah is adopted. Sounds so simple.

Two years later baby Jenna. Adopted.

What mess. What damage. What pain. What love. What help?

And some of them that meet Yvonne see the anger, just the anger, the violence and the pain. The mess. The dangerous veering from the norm.

And some see beyond.

What follows is taken from a card sent about Yvonne from a maternity nurse.
(On the front of the card is a picture of a squirrel eating an acorn.)

"I never had any dealings with Yvonne when she actually delivered her babies. We only met when she was admitted in early labour during the night!

One occasion there was a message from ambulance control - could they be met as they were coming in with a police escort as they had a very unco-operative patient on board. One Yvonne. So, as I stood in hospital reception, two burly policemen ran in saying I would need more help and security. I said I don't think so - Yvonne was delighted to see me, and as usual was easily persuaded to come with me by the offer of a cup of tea and some toast. So as we made our way up the stairs, me carrying her carrier bag and Yvonne starkers (for some reason) clutching the blanket from the ambulance, we chatted and glanced back to see the two ambulance men and two policemen standing with their mouths open. Apparently Yvonne had been very unco-operative and they couldn't believe the change - if only they had tried the cup of tea ploy! It always worked for me when I admitted Yvonne.

I would then see which vacant room she would like to use. Her favourite room was the Father's Waiting Room! I think she viewed it as her own personal bedsit – after all it had a comfy settee, a toilet, a shower, a tv and a warm radiator. She would do all her washing, hang them to dry on the radiator, choose a channel, settle down with blankets then promptly call for her tea and toast. If we admitted anyone else, the husbands would have to sit on hard chairs on the landing – they never complained!

If one went along with Yvonne, she was a pleasure to look after. One of her favourite pastimes was collecting all the bars of soap on the ward and then throwing them at the consultant when he did his rounds. Another time, Yvonne was asked if her waters had broken. She promptly squatted down in the corridor and did a wee on the floor, It was never boring when Yvonne was around! Although at times she was incredibly difficult, there was always something special about her."

Note from the writer:

Thank you for reading this far (listening maybe).

I wonder now what this is.

This is many things.

For the writer, an offering, an engagement, a learning, an offering, words.

For the mother, a prayer. A prayer and a love.

For the friend, a kindness and a holding.

And it is for Yvonne. Something for Yvonne.

This is Yvonne...

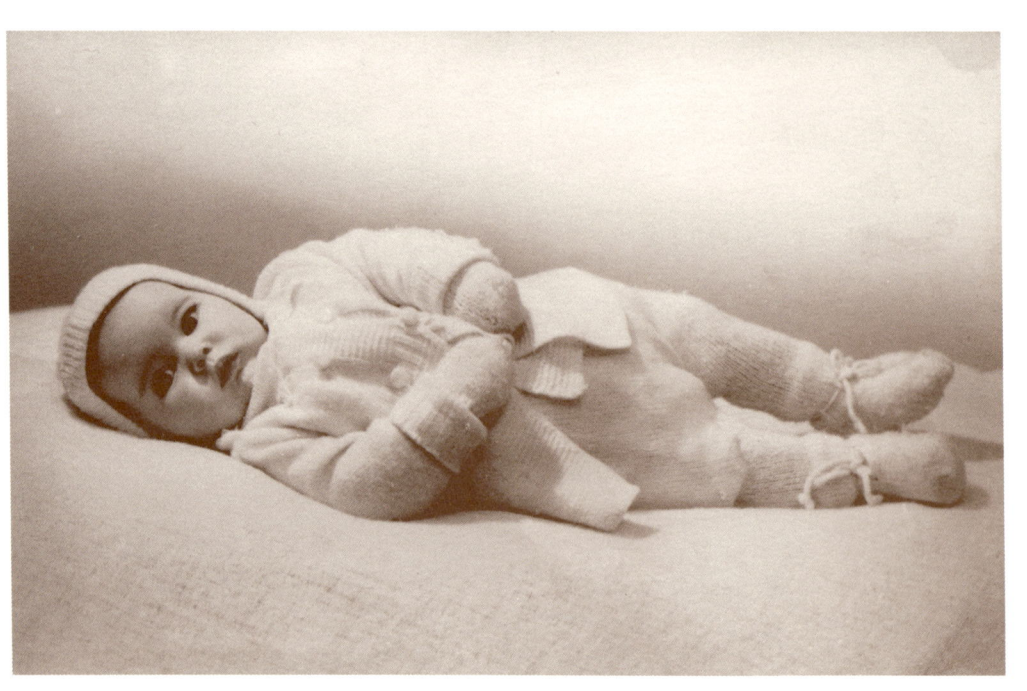

Yvonne loves her lost children with all of her heart. And few remember her grief. She is desperate now. More violent.

Personality disorder. Impossible to treat. Except with a spoonful of porridge.

Spells in cells. ¼ hour visits pushed to ½ hours. Pain in her face reflected by mine. Unreachable. And then another prison and she has to have a hysterectomy to stop cervical cancer and they take her to hospital and I can visit because there is goodness in the the kindness of a friend and the money given for my train ticket. Thank you Reggie.

And I see her and I am able to touch her and hold her and tell her I love her.

Then she is taken back to prison and I am not told. She gets more and more ill. We cannot get help. Nothing is appropriate.

Nothing is appropriate. Appropriate?

— • —

Yvonne is diagnosed with Schizophrenia. Finally some hope. She can see its an illness that is making her behaviour so bizarre. And some help? Some medication at least. But it's administered badly. She can hardly stand. She cannot hold her head up. Do you see? Can you see? Will you understand? She cannot hold her head up.

She gets married to David. They can only sustain it for 2 years. And finally Yvonne can go to live in a hostel, purpose built for those with mental health problems. Finally.

But she gets ill, her medication is wrong again, hospital, new doses. And she can go.
But the hostel can't have her back. Won't. She's a danger to herself and others. It's not appropriate. So she gets sent back into the community because she hasn't hurt anyone yet. She lives in a bed-sit. And Yvonne is vulnerable now. She gets her money at the post office and gives to the people she has met that go there with her. And she is loud. I think I would not like to live in the flat below her. She cannot cope in the community. She still does go to the clinic but now they take her off her medication. Disastrous. Months of extreme instability. She weeps in my arms.

She is diagnosed with Multiple Sclerosis. She gets so bad she can hardly move her legs. Bent up almost to her chest. Her world is pressing in on her. Not allowing her.

Death. Drugs. Promiscuity.
Personality Disorder. 6 adopted babies. Prisons.
Cervical Cancer. Hysterectomy. Schizophrenia.
Medication. Multiple Sclerosis.
Yvonne.

And now new difficulties. New brick walls for me to bang my head against.

I try to get her into a clinic for assessment of her MS but it's 'not appropriate'.
I try to get a neurological consultant for her privately but it's 'not appropriate'.
She hurts herself falling from bed in the care home, badly bruises her face.
But she can't have bed rails because of Health and Safety.
The type of injections she has are causing her legs to be worse.
She needs oral medication.
A wheelchair is made for her that doesn't fit, that causes her pain. She hardly uses it and the one time she does they think she's doing well.

Uphill struggles. Pillars to posts. Sidelined. Ridiculed. But most of all unseen. People see her conditions, her behaviour. They do not see Yvonne. A woman crying in physical pain; Yvonne's in a 'bad mood' they say.

We feel let down often by those that are meant to help. At times in her life, Yvonne tries to kill herself. And yet she keeps going.
'I am resigned' Yvonne says.

— • —

But Yvonne can see who cares. She can see the insides of people. And she is loved. And now there is more care for her, in the last months of her life. She has padded bed rails and a syringe device. She has regular visitors and family days. Marlene. Janet for Physio. And Nikki doing her nails and aromatherapy. And Jo doing her make-up. Making a fuss of her. Making her mean something. Seeing her.

Generous and accepting hearts. Just like Yvonne's. For her everyone is equal. Everyone is one.
Yvonne asks 'Can I pray for Myra Hindley?'

— • —

The pain is still there in her head and her limbs but there is a healing now. She smiles when we visit her. We are transformed in hope. The family. We are a family and we love each other. She teaches us, she makes us what we are. Her spirit, our spirits, rising above despair. Love. And laughter.

This is our inheritance. May 17th 2011.

Yvonne is dead.

She had a flat once. A new sofa. The place was spotlessly clean. And she prepared a beautiful meal for Barbara and me. She played a Rod Stewart cassette. And it was good.

— • —

On Mothering Sundays I give her a card and flowers. Yvonne gave life to six children.

I walk down to the peninsula where the land meets the sea and the sky, where Yvonne's ashes are with her father's grave.

And I hold, separate and place golden daffodils and the sun shines and the birds sing and a robin sits on her stone. Tiny fragile bird.

Hope. And the shatterings are made whole. We are at the edge of eternity. Held.

Yvonne, you were always part of our family. You always will be.

— • —

Yvonne's mum, Peggy:

"Darling Yvonne,

I have decided to write about you and your life, because I am very proud of you and how you overcame so much sadness. I can hardly imagine the pain you have suffered physically, mentally and spiritually. Sometimes I have had to step back from it because I can hardly bear to see what happened to you.

I am sorry for the times that I let you down, where fear took over and I had to withdraw. But you must know that I never stopped loving you and continue to love you now after death.

Love is so much stronger than fear. You taught me so much. You'll never know how much having you as a daughter meant to me, and to my ministry. You taught me to accept everyone as a child of God, you taught me not to be pre-decided about anyone, and to look for the essential person in the most difficult people. In many ways you have been a blessing not just to me but to many others.

The things that happened to you should be a lesson to us all; how we care for each other in a society that often seems only to be helpful to those that fit into a nice tidy box.

Not for you my darling. You were and remain a bright spark of independence in a world that looks for conformity at all costs, and the costs are dear for people like you. I pray that your life and the way that you coped so bravely will help others, both professional and lay, to come to a deeper understanding and compassion for those who have a mental illness."

In the midst of the darkness
Of the encircling gloom
Is the light
That is my daughter's
Unfailing love.

And the illness
That threatens to engulf her
And us
Cannot diminish ot tarnish
Such an amazing truth.

For this is the love
That has stood
The test of time and despair
And Shines
With the transcendance of hope.

Where would we be
If we had not
Known the anguish of heart,
For not to know the depth
Is not to know the height.

And my daughter's spirit
Is as free as could be
For her essential person
Though vulnerable and sometimes lost
Is held in the hand of God.

Though often ridiculed
And laid low
And put to scorn
Acquainted with sorrows
Too painful to say.

She bears the image of Christ
The marks of the nails
The wound in the side,
She shares with Him
The message of total love.

"Father forgive them,
They know not what they do",
And the world goes busily by
Never stopping to think,
There for Grace of God Go I.

By Peggy

A percentage of the proceeds from the sale of this book will be given to the:

Merlin MS Centre

'A place of support, therapy and information for Cornwall'

Telephone : 01726 885530   Email : hello@merlinmscentre.org.uk

Bradbury House
Hewas Water
Cornwall
PL26 7JF
Charity Number 1093691